Hostages

BY

Ed Hanson

THE BARCLAY FAMILY ADVENTURES

Development and Production: Laurel Associates, Inc.
Cover and Interior Art: Black Eagle Productions

SADDLEBACK
PUBLISHING·INC.
Three Watson
Irvine, CA 92618-2767

Website: www.sdlback.com

ISBN 1-56254-554-X

Printed in the United States of America
08 07 06 05   9 8 7 6 5 4 3 2 1

CONTENTS

MEET THE BARCLAYS

Paul Barclay
A fun-loving father of three who takes his kids on his travels whenever he can.

Ann Barclay
The devoted mother who manages the homefront during Paul's many absences as an on-site construction engineer.

Jim Barclay
The eldest child, Jim is a talented athlete with his eye on a football scholarship at a major college.

Aaron Barclay
Three years younger than Jim, he's inquisitive, daring, and an absolute whiz in science class.

Pam Barclay
Adopted from Korea as a baby, Pam is a spunky middle-schooler who more than holds her own with her lively older brothers.

CHAPTER 1

Planning the Trip

Jim woke up when he smelled bacon frying. Even if he'd forgotten today was Saturday, the aroma of bacon would have reminded him.

When his dad wasn't traveling, he always came by on Saturdays and made the family a big breakfast. Usually he made bacon or sausage, along with either eggs and hash browns or pancakes. It was a family ritual that Dad and Mom had agreed to keep going even though they were no longer together.

Jim looked at his watch. It was ten minutes to eight. He threw on some clothes and headed downstairs. He could hear his brother and sister talking in the kitchen. They were both laughing. *Dad's probably telling one of his corny jokes*, he thought to himself.

As he got nearer the kitchen the wonderful aromas got stronger. Jim smelled fresh bacon, hot coffee, and his favorite—buttermilk pancakes.

"Good morning, Jimbo," Paul Barclay said as Jim walked into the kitchen.

"Hi, Dad. What's everyone so happy about this morning?" he asked sleepily.

"Who wouldn't be happy with such a great breakfast coming up?" Paul said.

"And," Aaron added, "Dad was just telling us something exciting. He's been invited to Alaska to fish for king salmon and giant halibut!"

"Wow! That sounds like a fun trip. Are we going to go, too?" Jim asked.

"I don't see why not," Paul said. "I'm free now, and your spring vacation starts Monday. So what's to stop us?"

Jim looked at his younger sister. "How about you, Pam? Are you going?"

"No. I promised Mom I'd go with her

to visit Aunt Lily. Besides, I'd rather shop and go sightseeing than spend a week being cold and wet."

"Come on, Pam!" Aaron said.

"No, I really don't want to," Pam answered. "Sailing on a cruise ship might be okay, but I hate small boats. You can bring me back some salmon, though."

Aaron laughed. "We'll try our best to do that, Sis," he answered.

"Who do you know in Alaska?" Jim asked as he poured some juice.

"An engineer I worked with some time ago. Ben Roberts lives in Juneau—and he loves to fish. We've been talking about this trip for several years now," Paul answered.

Paul put the bacon on a plate. Then he took a tall stack of pancakes out of the oven and placed them on the table. "Okay, guys, dig in!" he said with a grin.

"Don't forget the maple syrup!" Aaron shouted.

Paul smiled and reached into the

cupboard. "Oh, yeah—no way we can forget that," he said as he placed a bottle of syrup on the kitchen table.

Moments later, Ann, the kids' mother, walked into the room.

"How do you expect anyone to sleep when you're making all this noise?" she said with a smile.

Pam laughed and said, "Sit down and have some pancakes, Mom."

"Just some coffee will be fine with me right now," Ann answered.

"Guess what, Mom?" Aaron chimed in. "Dad's going to take us to Alaska on a fishing trip!"

"Yes, I overheard you guys talking," his mother replied.

"But I'm not going, Mom," Pam said. "I'm going with you."

"Good," Ann answered. "You'll have a better time with us than you'd have on a smelly, old fishing boat anyway."

After breakfast Paul went into his office. First, he phoned the airlines to reserve tickets. Then he called his friend Ben in Juneau. Ben was delighted to hear about his old friend's plans. He quickly agreed to pick them up at the airport.

"What do we need to bring for an ocean fishing trip?" Paul asked.

"Just your clothes," Ben replied. "I'll charter the boat and stock it with food. I already have all the fishing gear that we'll need. But be sure to bring some *warm* clothes, Paul. It can get pretty chilly off the coast of Alaska—even in springtime."

"Sure thing, Ben! We'll see you on Monday about 5 o'clock."

CHAPTER 2

The *Neptune*

The trip to Juneau took most of the day. After flying to Seattle, Washington, the Barclays took an Alaska Airlines flight to Juneau. When they walked into the terminal at 5 o'clock, a booming voice shouted at them. "Welcome to Alaska!"

Paul turned around and saw Ben Roberts walking toward him. The man was grinning from ear to ear.

"Hi, Ben," Paul said as he hugged his old friend. "These are my two sons, Jim and Aaron."

Both boys reached out to shake hands with Ben.

"Hello, Mr. Roberts," they said to him. "Thank you for inviting us."

Ben took a step back, faking surprise.

"*Mr.* Roberts! Who's he? *My* name is Ben! If you guys call me Mr. Roberts again, I'll have to toss you in the ocean."

Jim and Aaron both laughed.

"Okay, you've got it, Ben," Jim assured him. "We sure don't want to end up as giant icicles!"

"Smart thinking, lads! The water up here is pretty darn cold. Well, let's get your bags. Then we can head down to the boat and get everything stowed."

"Sounds good to me," Paul agreed.

On the way to the docks, Ben drove past the Mendenhall Glacier, one of Juneau's main tourist attractions.

"Hey! I read about the Mendenhall Glacier in school," Jim said. "Isn't it the most visited glacier in the world?"

"You're right, Jim," Ben answered. "That's because it's so close to Juneau. It's an easy trip for tourists. At its center, the ice in the Mendenhall Glacier is more than 200 feet thick!"

"Wow!" Aaron cried. "That's really a

heck of a lot of thick ice!"

"It sure is, son," Ben said. "And did you know the glacier is slowly melting as it moves closer to the sea? Someday—not in our lifetimes, to be sure—this enormous glacier will be gone."

"Unless we have another ice age," Aaron piped up.

"I guess you're right, Aaron. Another ice age *would* change things. But do you really think that's very likely to happen anytime soon?" Ben asked.

"I don't know—I suppose not, Ben," Aaron responded.

Ben turned to Paul and said, "I've got the boat stocked for six days at sea. Do you think you'll want to stay out any longer than that?"

"No, I don't think so, Ben," Paul answered. "The boys have to be back at school next week."

"How about it, Ben? Do you think we'll catch any fish?" Jim asked.

"Well, son," Ben answered, "there are

no guarantees in hunting and fishing. But everything is in our favor. I expect that we'll do very well."

"I'd love to catch a giant halibut," Aaron said. "What are my chances?"

Smiling, Ben said, "I'm pretty sure we'll catch some halibut, Aaron. But catching a *shooter* is another story."

Aaron and Jim looked at each other with puzzled expressions on their faces.

"What's a *shooter*?" Jim asked.

"Oh, that's just an expression we use up here for halibut that weigh more than 90 or 100 pounds," Ben said. "We usually have to shoot those big boys when we get them to the water's surface. Halibut of that size are a solid mass of muscle. In fact, shooters have been known to break a fisherman's ankle as they thrash around on the deck. I keep a handgun on board just in case we hook one."

Both Jim and Aaron tried to imagine what it would be like to catch—or even to *see*—a fish that large. Ten minutes later

Ben parked the car at the marina. He led the Barclays to the far end of the pier where the *Neptune* was tied up.

"There she is, lads!" Ben shouted out proudly. "She'll be your home for the next five or six days!"

The *Neptune* was a 32-foot Nordic tug. Being relatively new, the boat was in good condition. She had a big diesel engine and carried 275 gallons of fuel. That gave her a cruising range of about 600 miles. Since she also carried 160 gallons of fresh water, five or six days at sea should be no problem at all.

In the bow of the boat, Ben pointed out a good-sized cabin with four bunk beds. He suggested that the two boys sleep there and use the two spare bunks for storage.

The pilothouse was in the center of the boat. It was next to the main cabin, which doubled as a kitchen and dining area. The Barclays noticed that the well-equipped kitchen had a refrigerator, freezer, and a two-burner propane stove complete with an oven.

Ben and Paul would sleep on two pull-down bunks in the main cabin. Aft of the main cabin was an open area on the deck for fishing.

For a while, the fishermen were busy stowing all their gear in the *Neptune*. Then the little group headed out to buy their fishing licenses and have dinner.

"We could eat aboard the *Neptune* tonight," Ben explained. "But since we'll be doing that for the next several days, let's go out tonight."

It was 10 o'clock that night when Ben Roberts and the Barclays finally crawled into their bunks. The boys were surprised that it was still daylight!

CHAPTER 3

Under Way at Last

The noisy diesel engine started up at 6 o'clock the next morning, and the *Neptune* motored away from the dock. The big engine's roar awakened Jim and Aaron out of a deep sleep. Both boys dressed quickly and ran up on deck. They found Ben Roberts in the pilothouse, steering the boat out of the harbor.

Ben chuckled when he saw them peering at him.

"Don't want to miss anything, do you, boys?" Ben said.

"Well, it's not that, Mr. Roberts—uh—I mean Ben. Oh, heck, I guess you're right," Jim answered.

"Just look around at this scenery, boys! Have you ever seen anything more beautiful?" Ben asked cheerfully.

They had no argument with their host's opinion. The snow-covered peaks and dense green trees were *spectacular*! Leaving Juneau by boat was a real treat.

"How long before we'll get our lines in the water, Ben?" Jim asked.

"Oh, we should be fishing in about three or four hours," Ben answered. "We have to go around Admiralty Island first. There's a large population of brown bears living out there. If you keep your eyes open, you might be able to see a bear or two along the shoreline."

Paul stuck his head into the pilothouse.

"Good morning, boys," he said. "Who wants to help me get breakfast going?"

Aaron was hungry. "I'll give you a hand, Dad," he volunteered.

A short time later, everyone had finished a hearty breakfast and cleaned up the dishes. Then the fishermen all sat back to enjoy the magnificent landscape.

Now they were only about half a mile off Admiralty Island, cruising along at about 12 knots. The *Neptune* was a solid, seaworthy fishing boat, but speed was not her strong suit.

The boys were excited to see several sea lions, a humpback whale with her baby, and bald eagles too numerous to count.

"Just seeing this beautiful, unspoiled country is worth the trip," Paul said.

"Well, I don't know about that, Dad," Aaron answered. "Don't forget that we came up here to catch fish."

Ben winked at Aaron. "And catch fish we will," he promised.

It was just about 10 o'clock when Ben put the engine in neutral.

"Time to break out the fishing rods, men," he said.

Then Ben started to climb atop the main cabin toward the storage area, where much of the gear was stowed. Anxious to help, Jim followed him.

Ben handed Jim several rods and said, "Pass these down to your dad."

Next came a tackle box, then a large net, and finally a small cooler stocked with herring.

After all the equipment had been passed down to Paul and Aaron, Jim noticed three more fishing rods in the storage area. They were much heavier than the others. These rods were as thick as broomsticks, and they were fitted with massive reels.

Jim was curious. "What are those rods for?" he asked Ben.

"Oh, those are the heavyweight rods that we use for halibut," Ben answered.

"They look like they could bring in a *whale*," Jim laughed.

"Well, remember, Jim—halibut up here can weigh up to 200 pounds—or even more! As you can guess, you need a real heavy rod for a fish that big."

When Ben and Jim got back to the main deck, Paul and Aaron had rigged several rods for trolling. Herring was the bait of choice, and Ben had plenty of it packed in ice.

The Barclays were feeling very lucky indeed. It was a beautiful day to be fishing off the coast of Alaska! The sun was shining brightly, and the air temperature was in the mid-50s. A slight sea was running. That made the *Neptune* roll gently—but not enough to cause any discomfort.

Paul went into the pilothouse and put the engine in gear. When the *Neptune* was under way, Ben showed the boys how to let out their lines. First, they released about 100 feet of line. Then they set the drag on their reels and placed each rod in a rod holder.

Ben nodded approvingly and said, "That's it, boys. Now all we have to do is wait for a fish to take the herring. When a fish hits, the rod will bend way over. That's when you grab the rod and start to reel in the salmon.

"I'm going up to talk with your dad for a while. Oh, and there's one last thing—when you get a strike, yell up to the pilothouse so we can stop the engine."

Ben left the Barclay kids on the stern of the boat. Each boy was staring intently at the two fishing rods, eagerly awaiting the first strike.

CHAPTER 4

Mystery Boat

Monday night was dark and still. About 20 miles off the Alaskan coastline, a large freighter came to a stop. The captain turned the freighter broadside to the sea. That positioning created a calm on the starboard side.

Then the ship's crane swung a 36-foot fishing boat over the side and slowly lowered it into the water. On board, there were three men, some fishing gear, and six very large coolers.

Nothing looked suspicious. Any other ships passing nearby would assume these were sport fishermen out for salmon. But they would be wrong!

As soon as the fishing boat was free, the freighter turned and headed out to sea. It was nearly 2 o'clock in the morning when the men on the fishing boat started the engine and headed due east. Now the boat was pointed directly toward the southern tip of Baranof Island.

The men on board had made careful plans. They would round the island just before daylight. By noon, they expected to be fishing off of Admiralty Island.

But sometimes, fate changes even the best-laid plans. . . .

CHAPTER 5

The First Fish

Aboard the *Neptune*, 40 minutes had gone by without any action.

"Gee, Jim," Aaron started to complain, "maybe we won't catch any—"

But before he could finish his sentence, the rod on the port side of the boat bent in half!

Jim grabbed the rod and pulled it from the rod holder.

"Dad, we have a fish on the line!" Aaron yelled up to the pilothouse.

Paul quickly put the engine in neutral. Then he and Ben hurried back to watch Jim try to land his first fish.

"Aaron, you'd better reel in that other line," Ben said. "If you don't, Jim's fish may get tangled up in it."

Aaron pulled the other rod from the holder immediately. Then he started to reel in the line while Jim was struggling with the thrashing salmon.

At one point, Jim had the fish within 10 feet of the boat. But then it turned and sped off like lightning! In just seconds, it pulled 50 feet of line off the reel. Finally, the tiring fish once again had come close to the *Neptune*'s stern. This time, Ben quickly put the net in the water and scooped up Jim's first salmon!

For a moment, the fishermen stood on deck admiring their catch. Then Ben said, "That's a nice fish, Jim—about 30 pounds, I expect. But we won't catch any more standing here. Paul, if you'll go up and get the *Neptune* under way, I'll get these lines back in the water."

The good fishing was steady all day. By about 5 o'clock that afternoon, they'd hooked five more salmon and landed three of them. Aaron caught the largest fish of the day—a 45-pounder.

As Ben filleted the fish and packed them in ice, he said, "Good work, guys! This has been quite a day. We have close to 80 pounds of fillets iced down already. You guys have *got* to be tired. Let's reel in the lines now and head to a mooring for the night."

"That's fine with us," Paul responded.

"Okay," Ben said. "There's a nice little protected cove a few miles down the coast. While I'm heading that way, you guys can clean off the salmon gear and put it away. Tomorrow, we'll go out after some of those giant halibut I've been telling you about."

It took half an hour to reach Funder Bay. When they arrived, they noticed several mooring buoys in the bay. Ben eased the *Neptune* alongside one of them.

Paul slipped a line around the buoy. Then he wrapped the other end to a cleat on the bow of the boat. Once the *Neptune* was safely tied up for the night, Ben shut down the engine.

Everyone was starving, so they lost no time making dinner. Over a meal of fresh salmon and rice, Ben said, "Tomorrow's fishing will be completely different."

"How's that?" Aaron asked.

"Well, son, in the first place, we'll be anchored and fishing on the bottom. I expect we'll be in 150 feet of water—maybe more. It takes a lot of work to pull up a large halibut from that depth."

"No wonder the reels on those other rods are so big," Jim said.

"That's right," Ben answered. "But remember that the *reel* doesn't do the work—the rod does. I'll show you what I mean tomorrow."

It was 10 o'clock at night now. Although it was still daylight, the fishermen were weary. All of them were glad to climb into their bunks for the night.

The next morning, the roar of the diesel engine once again jolted Jim and Aaron awake. When they came up on deck, they found an overcast day with a slight rain falling. They waved at Ben as he was carefully backing the *Neptune* away from the mooring buoy.

"Good morning, lads! Did you sleep well? Are you ready to catch some halibut today?" he called out.

"We sure are!" the Barclay boys both answered at once.

"Great! Why don't you two go back aft now and see if you can help your dad," Ben suggested.

On the stern, Paul was busy with the three heavy halibut rods.

"Morning, guys," he called out when he saw his boys.

"Hi, Dad! What are those red balls tied to the end of the line?" Aaron asked.

"Those are weights. In deep water, you need weights to carry your bait to the bottom. These particular weights are five-pounders. I think that should be enough. But we can always add more if we have to."

About 20 minutes later, Ben shut

down the engine. He went up on the bow to drop the anchor.

"We're in about 160 feet of water!" he yelled down to the boys.

Back on the stern, Ben smiled at the Barclays' eager faces.

"Now pay attention while I show you how we fish for halibut," he said.

He lowered one line into the water. The boys knew the water was very deep. But they were still surprised at how long it took for the five-pound weight to hit bottom.

"Now, watch!" Ben went on. "You *lightly* bounce the weight off the bottom. This kind of gentle movement is called 'jigging.' If a fish takes your bait, you'll know it. The pull will feel like a whole lot more than five pounds on the line."

Paul and the boys jigged the lines for about 15 minutes. Then Aaron said, "I think my line is snagged on the bottom, Ben. It seems stuck."

Ben let out a loud, hearty laugh.

"Son, that's a *halibut*! Are you ready? Now the hard work begins," he said.

Aaron was excited. He tried to reel in the line, but it didn't seem to move.

Ben reached out for Aaron's rod and said, "Let me show you. Remember what I said? You need to make the *rod* do the work—not the reel!"

Ben lifted the heavy rod until the tip pointed toward the sky. Then, as he lowered the tip back toward the water, he reeled in all the slack line.

"You have a real good-size halibut hooked, Aaron," Ben said. "It's going to take you some time to bring him all the way up from 160 feet."

Ben handed the rod back to Aaron. Then the determined teenager began the slow process of reeling in his fish. About 20 minutes later, Aaron was exhausted. But he had a 35-pound halibut thrashing at the surface of the water!

Ben quickly netted the fish, and they all watched it flapping on the deck of the

Neptune. Aaron's arms were tired. This halibut weighed only about 35 pounds. He wondered how *anyone* could reel in a 100-pounder!

The fishing was great all morning. By noon they'd landed five more halibut—all in the 25- to 35-pound range. As each catch was landed, Ben was kept busy filleting and packing it in ice.

A little after noon, Ben said, "Okay, guys. We now have about 150 pounds of fish iced down. I'd suggest that we get this fish taken care of before we try to catch any more."

Jim looked confused.

"What do you mean?" he asked.

"There's a fish-packing plant in the little village of Hoonah," Ben explained. "They'll freeze our fish for us and fly it down to Juneau. We can pick it up there when we return. Hoonah's only about 30 miles from here—just across Icy Strait. What do you say?"

"You're the boss, Ben," Paul said to

him with a big smile. "Let's go!"

By 1 o'clock the fishermen had stowed all their gear, pulled anchor, and set a course for Hoonah. They noticed that a strong wind had picked up. The seas in Icy Strait were getting rough.

As the *Neptune* plowed through the waves, it began taking water over the bow. Both Jim and Aaron started to feel their first pangs of seasickness.

Finally, at 5 o'clock that afternoon, the exhausted crew of fishermen arrived in Hoonah. Each and every one of them was happy to be out of the pounding sea.

Chapter 6

Uninvited Guests

Jim and Aaron were especially glad to be spending the night docked at Hoonah. Being on land gave them a chance to get some exercise. Life aboard a boat could get pretty confining.

The next morning the boys went out jogging for a couple of miles. By the time they got back to the *Neptune,* breakfast was ready.

Over bacon and eggs, Aaron asked, "What will we do today, Ben?"

"Well, we had mighty good luck off of Admiralty Island," Ben answered. "So, I'd suggest that we go back there. And on our way, we have to go right by a small bay where I've had good luck in the past. If no one objects, we could try some bay fishing for a couple of hours."

Paul saluted his friend. "Whatever you say, Ben. You're the captain," he said with a twinkle in his eye.

"Aaron and I will clean up the dishes," Jim volunteered. "Then let's get out of here and catch some more fish!"

Not long after leaving Hoonah Harbor, the *Neptune* crew was entertained by a surprise visit from a large school of dolphins. The playful creatures swam under, alongside, and in front of the boat. The fishermen admired their sleek bodies as they leapt in and out of the water. It was an unforgettable display of speed and grace! The show lasted for 20 minutes. Then the dolphins disappeared.

"They're probably off to entertain another boat," Ben said with a chuckle.

By mid-morning they were trolling herring again. After two hours with no strikes, Ben said, "Well, it looks like nobody's home today. I guess all the fish have gone to Admiralty Island. Let's pull these lines and head back over there."

Since the winds had subsided during the night, the seas in Icy Strait were much calmer than they had been the day before. The *Neptune* was just about half way across the strait when Paul spoke up.

"Aaron, will you hand me those binoculars?" he asked. "I think someone might need our help."

Paul peered through the binoculars for a moment.

"There's a boat off to our left," he said to Ben. "One of the men aboard seems to be waving at us. Take a look, Ben. Tell me what you make of it."

Looking through the glasses, Ben said, "I think you're right, Paul. Maybe they're in some sort of trouble. We'd better head over that way and see if we can give them a hand."

As the *Neptune* got closer, Paul could see three men on board. All of them were dressed in dark gray clothing that almost matched the color of their boat. Two had mustaches. None of their faces showed a hint of friendliness. Paul didn't like the looks of them. He had misgivings about approaching the boat. But before he could express his concerns to Ben, the *Neptune* had pulled alongside. Paul waved at the three men.

"Hello, there! What seems to be the trouble?" he shouted.

"Our engine just quit on us. Can you tow us into shallow water where we can anchor?" came the reply.

The two boats were now only a few feet apart. Suddenly, the strange men leaped aboard the *Neptune* and pulled out handguns! Without explanation, the armed men ordered Ben, Paul, and the boys to lie down on the deck!

While one man kept his gun aimed at them, the other two quickly transferred six large coolers to the *Neptune*'s deck. The coolers were obviously very heavy, because the men had to struggle to get them from one boat to the other.

Ben was outraged.

"Just a minute there! What's this all about?" he demanded.

The man with the gun didn't answer. In just a few minutes, everything they'd wanted from the disabled boat had been transferred to the *Neptune*. Then one man went back aboard and opened the boat's drain plugs to let in the sea water! Paul watched in amazement. Why would these three men want to sink their own boat? What could possibly be their purpose?

As her hull filled with sea water, the gray fishing boat began riding deeper and deeper in the water.

Finally, one of the hijackers said, "She's going down! Let's get out of here!"

Staring at the man who had just spoken, Paul couldn't help speaking up. "Would you mind telling us what's going on here?"

"You ask too many questions," the man snapped.

Two of the men explored the *Neptune* while one stayed with their captives. His handgun was always pointing in their direction. When the two men came back from scoping out the boat, one of them spoke to the armed man.

"Put them all in the forward cabin and lock the door," he ordered. "There's only one entrance to the cabin, so there's no way they can get out."

Ben, Paul, and the boys were quickly ushered into the forward cabin. The door was locked behind them. Moments later they heard the *Neptune*'s engine roar to life, and they were under way.

Peering out the small porthole, Ben said, "It looks like they're heading across Icy Strait toward Admiralty Island."

Until now, Jim and Aaron had been too terrified to speak.

Then Jim asked, "What do you suppose this is all about, Dad? And who *are* these guys?"

"I wish I knew, son. But I can tell you

this—I sure don't like our situation. All we can do now is stay as calm as possible and try to think."

CHAPTER 7

Captured

Aaron sat on the floor, staring at the locked cabin door. Then he got up and whispered to his father.

"Dad, those three guys are talking in the pilothouse," he said. "And look—the bottom of the cabin door is louvered. If we're all quiet, I may be able to hear what they're saying."

"Good idea, son. We won't utter a sound. Now go ahead and give it a try," said his father.

Aaron quietly moved to the door. He knelt down, pressed his ear against the louvers, and listened.

"Of all the lousy luck!" one of the men was complaining. "Our engine decides to quit on us."

"Yeah, but at least we got another boat," a second man said. "We can't let this affect our mission."

"We'll get the explosives to Juneau in time to meet our contact," the third voice said. "But what are we going to do with those guys in the forward cabin?"

For a moment there was silence. Then a voice growled, "We don't have much choice. We have to get rid of them."

"Wait a minute!" another man cried. "I didn't agree to murder. Blowing up the pipeline is one thing, but killing four people—that's another story."

"Look, I don't like it either," the first voice came back. "But what else can we do? We certainly can't take them back to Juneau with us."

Aaron decided that he'd heard enough. He walked quietly to the other side of the cabin where Paul, Ben, and Jim were anxiously waiting.

"Well, son?" Paul asked. "Did you learn anything?"

"I sure did—and it's all bad," Aaron answered. "First of all, these guys are some sort of terrorists. They're planning on blowing up the Alaskan pipeline! Those coolers they brought on board must be filled with explosives. And secondly— they plan on getting rid of us before heading back to Juneau."

"Oh, my God!" Ben said in a hoarse, strained voice. "This is serious."

"It sure is," Paul said, "so we can't just sit here like sheep. Ben—didn't you tell us that you'd brought a gun with you?"

"Yeah, I sure did," Ben replied. "It's right there in my duffel bag on the top bunk. But think about it, Paul—just one gun against three terrorists—those odds aren't very good!"

"No, they aren't," Paul agreed, "unless we can get an edge by surprising them."

"But we're locked up in the cabin!" Jim chimed in. "How are we going to surprise anybody?"

"Wait a minute!" Ben said. "There

may be another way out of this cabin besides the louvered door. See that wooden panel over there? It separates this cabin from the anchor locker in the bow of the boat. It's not a large compartment—just big enough to hold the anchor and 300 feet of line. But I just remembered that it has a hatch that opens onto the main deck."

"What if we took the panel off?" Paul asked. "If we pulled the anchor and line out, would there be enough room for one of us to get up to the main deck?"

Ben thought about it. "Maybe," he said. "Getting through that little hatch onto the main deck is the problem, Paul. Aaron might make it—but I don't think the rest of us could."

"Well, let's give it a try," Paul said. "Ben, while the boys and I remove the panel, you get your gun. And make sure that it's loaded!"

Six screws held the panel in place. It wasn't hard to remove them. Then,

slowly and quietly, Paul and the boys
began pulling the anchor line into the
cabin.

Next, Paul and the boys carefully
removed the anchor and placed it on one
of the bunks. Ben had been right. A full-
grown man could never make it through
the hatch. Aaron was their only hope!

Paul sat back on one of the bunks.
Ben noticed the worried look on his face.
He reached out and patted Paul's arm.

"I know what you're thinking, old
friend," Ben said. "It seems like an awful
lot to ask of a kid."

"How can I do such a thing, Ben?"
Paul asked. "I can't expect a young boy to
go out there on his own and face three
armed terrorists. It's crazy!"

Aaron was listening closely to the
conversation.

"Dad," he said, "I know I'm just a kid.
But if you'll just tell me what needs to be
done, *I'll do it.*"

Paul put his arm around his son and

hugged him. Jim thought he saw a tear rolling down his father's cheek.

Finally, Paul sighed. Then he said, "Good man, Aaron! Here's the plan."

CHAPTER 8

Escape Plan

Ben and the three Barclays huddled together in the forward cabin as Paul laid out their plan.

"As soon as it's dark, Aaron will enter the anchor locker," Paul said. "Then he'll go through the hatch up onto the main deck. *Aaron—you must not make a sound.* Surprise is our only hope. Crawl along the deck and into the pilothouse. Then unlock the door to this cabin. If they're still in the main cabin, I think you can get by them without being seen."

"What happens then?" Jim asked.

"I'll crawl along the port side to the fishing area in the stern," Paul continued. "You can time me, Ben. Give me about two minutes to get there. Then

46

burst into the main cabin with your gun in hand. When I hear you, I'll rush through the rear door to help. With any luck, we can overpower them before they can figure out what's happening."

"But what can *I* do?" Jim asked.

"Not much, I'm afraid. Just pray that our plan works," Paul answered.

The three uninvited guests were eating and drinking in the main cabin. From the sound of their laughter, they seemed to be in good spirits.

Aaron eased his body into the anchor locker. Then he quietly pushed open the hatch cover to the main deck.

He was glad to see that the sun had gone down. In the cover of darkness, he wriggled his shoulders through the narrow opening. It was a tight squeeze, even for him. After closing the hatch behind him, he inched along the deck toward the pilothouse.

Aaron's heart was pounding! He wondered if everyone on board could hear it. But as frightened as he was, he knew that the success of their plan depended on him! He *had* to keep going. At last he reached the pilothouse and crawled in on his stomach.

He stared at the louvered door in horror. The key wasn't in the lock! No one had thought of that! If one of the men had put the key in his pocket, their plan was ruined.

Aaron's mind was racing. He tried to think where they might have put the key. Maybe they threw it on the ledge above the steering wheel. But he'd have to stand up to look there.

He slowly rose to his feet. Now he could see the three men in the main cabin. A chilling shudder went through his whole body! Then he glanced at the ledge and saw a key off to one side! He grabbed the key and dropped back to his knees. He prayed it was the key that fit the louvered door.

Aaron eased the key into the lock and

turned it. He heard a light clicking noise, and the door swung open.

"Mighty good work, Aaron," his father whispered. "Now go back there and hide with Jim."

Paul looked over at Ben.

"Looks like it's showtime. Are you ready, Ben?" he asked.

"Yes, Paul. You bet," Ben answered. "I'll give you two minutes to get to the stern before I make my move."

As Paul began making his way toward the stern, Aaron and Jim looked at each other. Not a word was spoken, but each boy knew what the other was thinking. *Their very lives depended on what happened in the next couple of minutes.*

As Paul disappeared quietly into the darkness, Ben gripped his handgun tightly. His palm was sweaty. The .357 Magnum felt as if it weighed 50 pounds.

Two minutes passed. It was time.

Ben crawled silently into the pilothouse. In one swift motion, he threw open the door to the main cabin.

"Hands up! I'll shoot the first person who moves!" he shouted.

At exactly the same moment, Paul burst through the rear door. He picked up a fish gaff and waved it over his head threateningly.

The three men were completely taken by surprise! They didn't move. Paul took their weapons while Ben kept his gun trained on them.

Less than 15 minutes later, all three intruders were bound hand and foot and tied to a railing. For the first time since the terrorists had come on board, Ben, Paul, and the boys could relax.

Ben got on the radio and called the coast guard station in Juneau. After reporting in detail what had happened, he asked them to send help. He and Paul were eager for the coast guard to take the prisoners off their hands.

Ben turned to Paul as he clicked off the radio.

"A coast guard cutter will be here in about three hours," he said, breathing a great long sigh of relief.

The fishermen felt drained as they sat in the cabin, awaiting the coast guard.

A short time later, Jim spoke up. "We did all right, guys. Maybe we didn't get any salmon or halibut today," he said, "but it looks like we caught ourselves some even bigger fish!"

CHAPTER 9

Coast Guard Help

It was 7 o'clock in the morning when the coast guard cutter pulled alongside the *Neptune*. Lt. Plummer took charge of transferring the prisoners and the coolers full of explosives. Then the lieutenant congratulated the *Neptune*'s crew on retaking their boat.

"Gosh, most of the credit should go to Aaron," Paul explained. "If he hadn't unlocked the door for us, we'd be their prisoners right now—if we were still alive, that is!"

Lt. Plummer smiled at Aaron. "Well, son," he said, "you should be mighty proud of yourself. As a matter of fact, I believe that your actions deserve a commendation. I'll certainly recommend

52

it to my superiors in the coast guard."

"Thank you, sir," Aaron replied.

"We still have a lot of work to do," Lt. Plummer went on. "Obviously, someone was going to meet these guys in Juneau. We'll stake out the dock there for the next few days. Every car or boat that looks suspicious will be thoroughly searched."

"You know, sir," Paul said, "I don't think the terrorists intended to move the explosives out of Juneau by car."

"No? What makes you say that?" Lt. Plummer asked.

"Think about it for a minute," Paul answered. "To reach the pipeline by car would mean taking the ferry from Juneau—probably to Skagway. That's not a problem.

"But driving from Skagway means crossing into Canada and then back into the United States. That would mean going through customs *twice*! And that wouldn't be a very smart move, would it? Not for guys who were carrying hundreds of pounds of dangerous explosives."

Lt. Plummer nodded. "You might have something there," he said.

"My guess is that they were going to *fly* the explosives out of Juneau," Paul continued. "I think the authorities there should be checking the airport."

"I'll pass that along," Lt. Plummer said. "Good luck with the rest of your fishing trip. And, Ben—be sure to radio us just before you head back in. I'll have someone meet you and update you on this case."

Ben shook his head.

"I don't know if we can concentrate on fishing after everything we've been through," he answered.

"Oh, sure you can! Once you get a big king salmon on your line, you'll forget all about your uninvited guests," Lt. Plummer said.

"I sure hope you're right," Paul replied with a smile.

As the coast guard cutter headed back

to Juneau, Ben got the *Neptune* under way. He headed the boat back to the area off of Admiralty Island where they'd been successful two days earlier.

They trolled for salmon until 4 o'clock that afternoon. Six fish hit their bait and three of them were boated. Lt. Plummer had been right. The excitement of fighting the huge king salmon made the experience with the terrorists seem like a distant memory.

Early that evening the fishermen began to realize how tired they were. No one had slept the night before. They'd been too busy planning and executing their escape. By 8 o'clock that night, all four of the weary fishermen were sound asleep in their bunks.

CHAPTER 10

Confession

At the Juneau police station, Lt. Plummer met with police officers. Four FBI agents had also been flown in to help on the case. The three prisoners had been questioned, but so far none of them had been willing to talk.

Special Agent Burns spoke out first. "Gentlemen, we got a lucky break when Ben Roberts and Paul Barclay were able to capture these terrorists. But I'm pretty sure these guys are small potatoes. We need to know who their contacts are. Who's *behind* all this?"

"You're right," Lt. Plummer agreed. "It looks like we can prevent *this* bombing— but they can always send someone else and try again."

"Give me 15 minutes alone with one of those guys," said a burly young police officer. "I'll find out everything we need to know."

Agent Burns looked at the young officer disapprovingly.

"In the United States, we don't beat confessions out of prisoners," he said.

"You're right—we don't do that," Lt. Plummer agreed. "But there's nothing wrong with trying to *trick* one of them into confessing."

"What do you mean?" Burns asked.

"Well, just before I left the *Neptune*, Paul Barclay suggested we check the airport. He thought they'd try to get out of Juneau by small plane. I think that's a good idea," Lt. Plummer said.

Burns frowned. "So, what does that do for us?" he asked. "What exactly do you have in mind?"

"What if we take the youngest man and try to convince him that his partners have betrayed him?" the lieutenant asked. "We know the pipeline is the target. If the small plane idea is correct, we can trick him into thinking that his partners told us all about it."

"Yeah," said Burns. "We'll tell him he has a choice. He can either cooperate with us and receive a light sentence—*or* spend the next 15 to 20 years locked up in prison."

"It might work—and it sure beats hanging around the airport for a whole week," one of the officers added.

Early the following morning, the youngest prisoner was brought into the interrogation room. Just 19 or 20 years old, the young man looked frightened. The bold attitude he'd displayed at his capture was now gone.

Agent Burns took the lead. "One of your buddies has told us the whole story. We know that your target was the pipeline. And we know that you were planning to leave Juneau by private plane. If you cooperate with us now, we can probably get you off with a light sentence. Otherwise, I'm afraid you can look forward to many years behind bars."

Before the terrified prisoner could answer, Lt. Plummer chimed in.

"Don't be a stubborn fool, son," he said. "You're a young man. Why waste the best part of your life in prison?"

The young man began to sob.

"I didn't really even want to do this!" he cried. "They talked me into it."

Once he started talking, they couldn't get him to stop. He told them the date and time they were to meet the plane at the airport. And he explained their plan to blow up three separate sections of the pipeline many miles apart.

He gave them the name of the freighter that dropped them off the Alaskan coastline. By the time he was finished, the authorities were satisfied. They had everything they needed to make numerous arrests and protect the flow of valuable crude oil.

CHAPTER 11

Hero's Reward

Two days later, the *Neptune* motored up to the dock in Juneau. Ben and the Barclays were surprised to see a group of people waiting on the dock.

Paul looked at Ben and said, "What do you suppose is going on?"

Ben shrugged. "Darned if I know," he answered.

After the mooring lines were secure, a small group of men, led by Lt. Plummer, came aboard.

"Gentlemen," the lieutenant said with a smile, "this is the mayor of Juneau. She has a special award for Aaron."

The mayor was holding a plaque, which she proceeded to read:

TO AARON BARCLAY
BECAUSE OF YOUR BRAVERY AND COURAGE,
AN ENVIRONMENTAL DISASTER OF MAJOR
PROPORTIONS WAS PREVENTED.
THE ENTIRE STATE OF ALASKA THANKS YOU.

It was signed by the governor.

Jim grinned and playfully punched his brother's arm.

"Wow!" he said teasingly. "Back home you're a nobody—but here in Alaska you're a real hero!"

Aaron ignored his brother, thanked the mayor, and proudly accepted the plaque. Everyone in the small crowd began to applaud.

Paul put his arm around Aaron and said, "I'm very proud of you, son."

Now it was Ben's turn to speak.

"Thank heaven you got through that hatch and unlocked the door. If you hadn't, we'd probably all be fish food by now! Thanks a million, Aaron," he said.

Just before leaving, the mayor said,

"The governor regrets not being here personally, Aaron. But he had to fly to Washington for a conference today."

Then Lt. Plummer took Paul and Ben aside. He quickly filled them in on the events of the past few days.

"We got all of them," he said. "Your suggestion about the small plane was right on target, Paul."

Paul shook the lieutenant's hand.

"I'm glad it worked out," he said. "The whole experience certainly added some excitement to our fishing trip."

"Yeah," Jim said, "Mom's never going to believe what happened on this trip. I can't wait to get home and tell her."

Paul smiled at his son and said, "Maybe it'd be a good idea to leave out some of the details, Jim—if you ever want to join me on another fishing trip, that is!"

COMPREHENSION QUESTIONS

Who and Where?

1. In what city and state did Ben Roberts live?

2. Near what island did Ben and the Barclays fish for salmon?

3. Which fisherman caught the first salmon?

4. Who listened in on the hijackers' conversation?

5. Where did Aaron find the key to the louvered door?

6. Who kept his gun trained on the hijackers?

Remembering Details

1. What famous tourist attraction did the Barclays visit in Juneau?

2. What was the name of Ben's Nordic tugboat?

3. What was the terrorists' ultimate goal?

4. What sea creatures gave the fishermen "an unforgettable display of speed and grace"?

5. Where did the terrorists keep their explosives hidden?

6. What did the hijackers do to their own disabled boat?

7. What valuable natural resource is carried by the Alaskan pipeline?